Rabbi Benjamin's Buttons

Alice B. McGinty ⬤ Illustrated by Jennifer Black Reinhardt iⁱⁱⁱi Charlesbridge

In memory of my
grandmother, Claire Karp,
who made the most scrumptious
matzoh-ball soup of all—**A. B. M.**

To Mom and Dad, for the gift of a loving
family—you are the sunshine of my heart—**J. B. R.**

First paperback edition 2017
Text copyright © 2014 by Alice B. McGinty
Illustrations copyright © 2014 by Jennifer Black Reinhardt
All rights reserved, including the right of reproduction in whole
or in part in any form. Charlesbridge and colophon are registered
trademarks of Charlesbridge Publishing, Inc.

Published by Charlesbridge
85 Main Street
Watertown, MA 02472
(617) 926-0329
www.charlesbridge.com

Library of Congress Cataloging-in-Publication Data
McGinty, Alice B., 1963–
     Rabbi Benjamin's buttons/Alice B. McGinty; illustrated by Jennifer Black Reinhardt.
          p. cm.
     Summary: Rabbi Benjamin's congregation presents him with a special holiday vest—
and cooks him so much food that soon its buttons pop off. Includes glossary, notes on
Jewish holidays, and recipes for special foods associated with them.
     ISBN 978-1-58089-432-6 (reinforced for library use)
     ISBN 978-1-58089-433-3 (softcover)
     ISBN 978-1-60734-747-7 (ebook)
     ISBN 978-1-60734-632-6 (ebook pdf)
1. Rabbis—Juvenile fiction. 2. Fasts and feasts—Judaism—Juvenile fiction. 3. Jewish cooking—
Juvenile fiction. [1. Rabbis—Fiction. 2. Fasts and feasts—Judaism—Fiction. 3. Holidays—Fiction.
4. Jewish cooking—Fiction.] I. Reinhardt, Jennifer Black, 1963- ill.
II. Title.
PZ7.M16777Rab 2013
813.54—dc23   2012038695

Printed in China
(hc) 10 9 8 7 6 5 4 3 2
(sc) 10 9 8 7 6 5 4 3

Illustrations done in watercolor and ink on Arches bright white
     300-lb. hot-press watercolor paper
Display type set in Blue Century by T-26
Text type set in Hunniwell by Aah Yes
Color separations by KHL Chroma Graphics, Singapore
Printed by 1010 Printing International Limited
     in Huizhou, Guangdong, China
Production supervision by Brian G. Walker
Designed by Whitney Leader-Picone

091929.5K3/B0725/A5

Rabbi Benjamin loved his synagogue on Walnut Street. With a warm, wide smile, he welcomed everyone who entered. "A happy congregation is the sunshine of my heart," the rabbi said.

"You are the sunshine of *our* hearts," the congregation told Rabbi Benjamin. That's why in the autumn, to celebrate the new Jewish year, they made the rabbi a special holiday vest, fastened in the front with four shiny silver buttons.

How the rabbi smiled when he put on that beautiful vest! It fit just right.

Dressed proudly in his new vest, Rabbi Benjamin led Rosh Hashanah services. After the shofar had sounded to welcome the New Year, everyone celebrated in the very best way: with lots of holiday food.

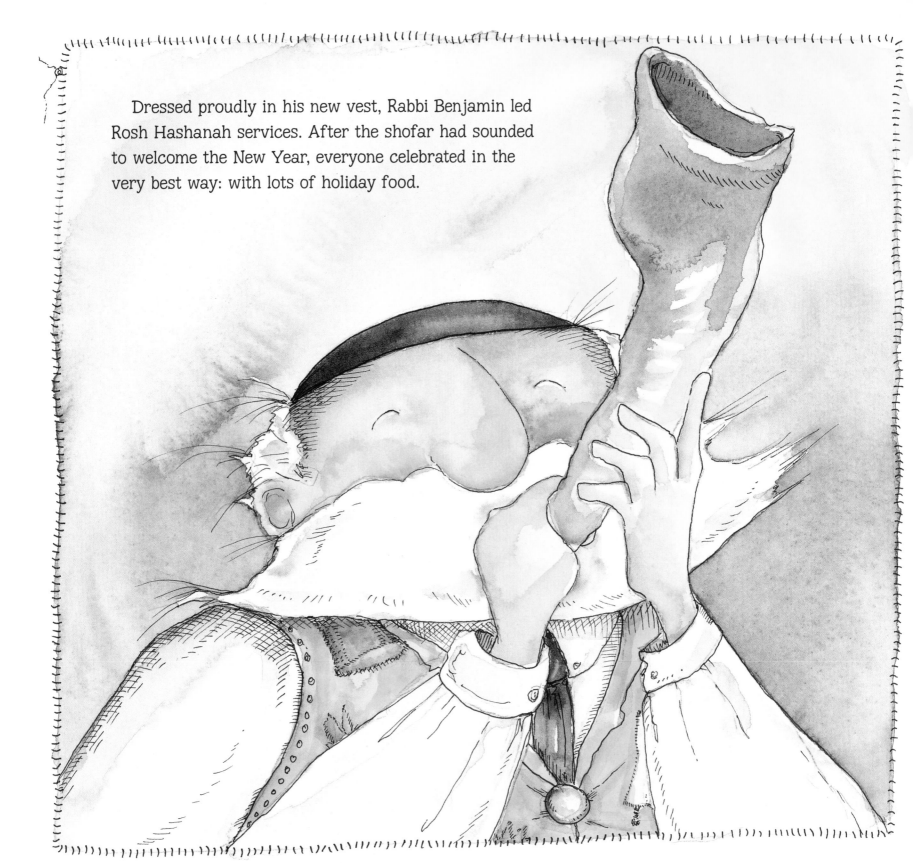

"Try my mama's apple torte," said Mrs. Bergman's youngest boy. When the rabbi did, oh, how Mrs. Bergman smiled. Mrs. Muchnik grinned when he praised her delicious honey cake. And the whole Goldwasser family glowed when he dipped slices of their homegrown apples into sweet, sweet honey.

Rabbi Benjamin rejoiced with his happy congregation and ate until his holiday vest stretched tightly across his belly.

During Sukkot, the autumn festival of the harvest, Rabbi Benjamin visited a different family's sukkah each night. Sitting in their sukkot under starry skies, they sang songs of thanksgiving and ate meals of squash, stuffed cabbage, and sweet-potato pie. The rabbi ate and sang until his holiday vest stretched *very* tightly across his belly.

It stretched so tightly that on the last day of Sukkot, after a slice of Mr. Hoover's fabulous fruit strudel—*pop!*—one of the four shiny silver buttons popped off and landed—*splat!*—in the etrog jelly. Rabbi Benjamin gasped and covered his belly with lulav leaves. Had anyone noticed?

The next day he fixed his vest with a good, strong pin.

In the winter came Chanukah, the Festival of Lights. To remember the miracle of the oil that burned in the ancient temple for eight days and nights, the congregation lit the menorah, spun the dreidel, and ate lots of latkes.

"Oy-yoy-yoy," the rabbi groaned. His vest stretched tight as he sampled latke after latke, the crispiest one of all fried by the three grinning Goldwasser girls. "Have another!" they chanted. So he did.

Then, on the last night of Chanukah, right in the middle of a blessing—*pop!*—it happened again. The second shiny silver button popped off and sank—*kerplunk!*—in the applesauce. Rabbi Benjamin gulped and hid behind the menorah. When he arrived home, he replaced the missing button with his very best tallis clips.

Soon it was spring and time to celebrate Passover. Rabbi
Benjamin sucked in his stomach and put on his holiday vest.
He buttoned the last two buttons, clipped the clips, pinned
the pin, and hoped for the best.

At the Goldwassers' house, they read from the Passover Haggadah, sang songs, and ate the traditional seder meal to remember when the Jewish people had been slaves.

How the Goldwasser girls flushed with pride when the rabbi said their charoset had just the right mix of apples and nuts. When Rabbi Benjamin spread horseradish on Mr. Muchnik's gefilte-fish patties, the littlest Muchnik smiled. And my, did Mrs. Bergman beam when the rabbi sipped her scrumptious matzoh-ball soup.

POP!
POP!

PLOP!

SPLISH-
SPLASH!

MATZOH

"A happy congregation is the sunshine of my heart," the rabbi said. He ate and ate until—*pop! pop!*—the last *two* shiny silver buttons popped off his vest. The first landed—*plop!*—in the horseradish. The second landed— *splish-splash!*—in the cup set aside for Elijah the prophet. The rabbi gasped and hid behind the matzoh box.

Rabbi Benjamin said a few quick good-byes and hurried home, frowning all the way.

"Oy-yoy-yoy. What a mess!" he cried. "I've ruined my special holiday vest!"

Rabbi Benjamin could have frowned all summer long,
but as he scrub, scrub, scrubbed his vest, he had an idea.
Rabbi Benjamin asked the Hoovers if he could help
plant their garden to make a big harvest for next Sukkot.

He helped Mrs. Bergman hide boxes of Chanukah presents from her boys.

He hiked with the Muchniks to the lake and caught carp for next Passover's gefilte-fish patties.

He helped the Goldwasser family harvest
homegrown apples for Rosh Hashanah.
The rabbi planted and picked and sweated
and fished all summer and into the autumn.

On the eve of Rosh Hashanah, Rabbi Benjamin took
out his holiday vest. He thought it would fit again, but
what about the missing buttons? He tried new pins to
fasten the vest, but it sagged. He tried tallis clips and tie
clips, but it scrunched. He tried string, and even staples,
but nothing worked.

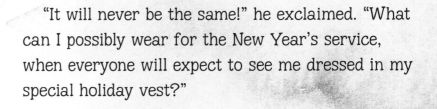

"It will never be the same!" he exclaimed. "What can I possibly wear for the New Year's service, when everyone will expect to see me dressed in my special holiday vest?"

It was then he heard a knock at his door. In marched the Goldwasser family, followed by the Hoovers, Mrs. Bergman and her boys, and all six Muchniks.

"You are the sunshine of our hearts," the Goldwasser girls told the rabbi.

"So we've brought you a New Year's gift," said the littlest Muchnik.

To: Rabbi Benjamin

The rabbi's eyes grew wide. Inside the box was a
brand-new holiday vest, even lovelier than the first.

And right in front were four very familiar shiny silver buttons.

That evening Rabbi Benjamin's smile was warm and wide as he welcomed his congregation to Rosh Hashanah services at the synagogue on Walnut Street.

"A happy congregation is the sunshine of my heart," the rabbi said. Such joy swelled in Rabbi Benjamin's chest that he *almost* popped a button on his brand-new holiday vest.

ROSH HASHANAH (ROSH hah-SHAH-nah)

Rosh Hashanah is the Jewish New Year, celebrated in the autumn. In Hebrew, "rosh hashanah" means "head of the year." Sweet foods such as honey cake or apple slices dipped in honey are eaten to symbolize the hope for a sweet new year.

Mrs. Muchnik's Delicious Honey Cake

Preparation time: 20 minutes. Baking time: 1 hour. Makes two loaves.

This recipe should be made with adult assistance and supervision.

Dry ingredients
2 cups flour
½ teaspoon baking soda
½ teaspoon baking powder
½ teaspoon salt
1 teaspoon cinnamon
1 teaspoon allspice

Other ingredients
½ cup vegetable oil
1 cup sugar
3 eggs
¾ cup honey
½ cup strong coffee (cold)

1. **Preheat** oven to 350°.
2. **Combine** all dry ingredients (flour, baking soda, baking powder, salt, cinnamon, and allspice) in a medium bowl and set aside.
3. **Cream** oil and sugar together in a large bowl.
4. **Beat** eggs lightly with a fork in a small bowl, then add them to the large bowl of oil and sugar. **Mix** thoroughly.
5. **Mix** in the honey and coffee.
6. **Add** the mixture of dry ingredients a bit at a time. **Mix** together.
7. **Bake** in two 9-by-5-inch loaf pans lined with waxed paper for approximately 1 hour.
8. **Test** if the cake is done by inserting a knife into it. If the knife comes out clean, the cake is ready!
9. **Cool** before serving.

SUKKOT (soo-KOHT)

Sukkot is the week-long Jewish festival of the harvest celebrated about two weeks after Rosh Hashanah. Sukkot is named after the huts that Jewish people lived in long ago when they wandered in the desert. The huts were also used in the fields by farmers when they harvested their crops. During Sukkot, people eat stuffed foods and fruits and vegetables from the harvest.

Mr. Hoover's Fabulous Fruit Strudel

This recipe has three parts. Preparation time: 3 hours. Baking time: 50 minutes. Makes two strudels.

This recipe should be made with adult assistance and supervision.

Dough ingredients

1 package dry yeast
¼ cup lukewarm water
3 egg yolks
2 tablespoons sugar
2 tablespoons sour cream
3 cups flour
½ teaspoon salt
1 cup room-temperature margarine
vegetable or olive oil, to coat bowl

Filling ingredients

3 large apples
2 plums
½ cup raisins
1 tablespoon lemon juice
1 cup sugar
½ cup fresh bread crumbs
¾ teaspoon cinnamon
¼ teaspoon salt

Dough

1. **Dissolve** yeast in lukewarm water in a medium bowl. **Let sit** for 10 minutes.
2. **Add** egg yolks, sugar, and sour cream. **Mix** well and set aside.
3. **Combine** the flour and salt in a large bowl. **Cut in** margarine with a pastry cutter or two crisscrossing butter knives until it forms pea-size crumbles.
4. **Stir** in egg mixture.
5. **Knead** the dough with your hands for a few minutes until smooth.
6. **Coat** a bowl with vegetable or olive oil and place the dough in the bowl.
7. **Refrigerate** for 2 hours. (Make the filling below while the dough is chilling.)

Filling

1. **Pare, core,** and **slice** the apples into thin slices. **Pit** and **slice** the plums.
2. **Put** the apples, plums, raisins, lemon juice, sugar, bread crumbs, cinnamon, and salt in a bowl. **Mix** well, coating the apples and plums thoroughly.

Once the dough has chilled for two hours

1. **Preheat** oven to 350°.
2. **Divide** the dough in half, and using a rolling pin, **roll** each half into a square.
3. **Place** half the filling on each square.
4. **Roll** the dough up, trapping the filling inside.
5. **Bake** for 50 minutes on an ungreased jelly-roll pan or cookie sheet.

CHANUKAH (HAHN-uh-kah)

Chanukah is the eight-day Jewish festival of lights and takes place in winter. The holiday celebrates the victory of Judah and the Maccabees against the Syrian army when they fought to defend their right to practice Judaism. When the Jewish people took back the temple in Jerusalem, they lit the eternal light using the tiny bit of oil left. While the messenger sent to get more oil was gone, a miracle happened. The tiny bit of oil lasted for eight days and nights until the messenger returned. Each evening during Chanukah, an additional candle is lit in the menorah to remember each night the oil lasted. People eat potato pancakes, called latkes, which are fried in oil and served with sour cream and applesauce.

The Three Goldwasser Girls' Crispy Potato Latkes

Preparation time: 30 minutes. Cooking time: 20 minutes. Makes 12–14 latkes.

This recipe should be made with adult assistance and supervision.

Ingredients

4 large potatoes
1 small onion
1 egg
½ teaspoon salt
¼ teaspoon pepper
1 tablespoon flour
1 teaspoon baking powder
½ cup olive oil for frying

1. **Peel** and **grate** the potatoes.
2. **Wrap** the potato gratings in cheesecloth, and **press** to remove most of the liquid.
3. **Chop** the onion.
4. **Mix** grated potato with chopped onion, egg, salt, pepper, flour, and baking powder in a bowl until a batter forms.
5. **Heat** oil in frying pan on medium heat.
6. **Spoon** batter into the hot oil, spreading to form 3-inch pancakes.
7. **Fry** until edges are browned.
8. **Lift** the latkes out with a spatula, and **place** them on a plate lined with paper towels to absorb excess oil.

PASSOVER

Passover, or Pesach (PAY-sahk), is an eight-day holiday that starts with a seder meal and includes the retelling of the Jewish people's freedom from slavery in Egypt. Special foods include horseradish as a reminder of the bitterness of slavery, parsley and eggs dipped in salt water as a reminder of the tears shed by the slaves, and matzoh to remember how the Jewish slaves fled from Egypt without time to let their bread rise before baking.

Mrs. Bergman's Magnificent Matzoh Ball Soup

This recipe has two parts. Preparation time: 1 hour. Cooking time: 2½ hours. Makes 8 servings.
This recipe should be made with adult assistance and supervision.

Soup ingredients

1–2 lbs. of boneless chicken breasts

8 cups water

½ teaspoon salt

3 stalks celery

1 parsnip

4 stalks parsley

1 medium onion

4 carrots

2 bay leaves

½ teaspoon pepper

thyme and more salt, to taste

Matzoh ball ingredients

2 tablespoons vegetable oil

2 large eggs, slightly beaten

½ cup matzoh meal

2 tablespoons stock from soup above

Soup

1. **Cut** raw chicken breasts into quarters.
2. **Put** chicken in pot with water.
3. **Bring to a boil,** and **remove** white residue from top.
4. **Add** salt, cover, and **simmer** for about an hour.
5. While the pot simmers, **chop** celery, parsnip, parsley, onion, and carrots.
6. **Add** the vegetables to the pot, then bay leaves, pepper, thyme, and salt to taste.
7. **Simmer** another 30 minutes.
8. **Strain** soup into another pot, **shred** the chicken, and **place** it back in the broth.
9. **Puree** vegetables in a blender. **Pour** vegetable puree back into soup and stir.

Matzoh balls

1. **Mix** oil, eggs, and matzoh meal together. **Add** soup stock until blended.
2. **Cover** and place in refrigerator for 15 minutes.
3. **Remove** from refrigerator.
4. **Make** balls of approximately one inch diameter by rolling the mixture between your hands.
5. **Bring** the soup to a boil, and one by one **drop** the balls into it.
6. **Cover** pot, and **simmer** for 30–40 more minutes.

GLOSSARY

charoset (hah-ROH-sit): a mixture of chopped apples, nuts, cinnamon, and wine eaten at Passover; it serves as a reminder of the mortar the slaves used when they built brick pyramids as Egyptian slaves

dreidel (DRAY-duhl): a small, four-sided spinning top used in a game of chance at Chanukah

Elijah's cup (eh-LIE-jahz KUP): a ceremonial cup of wine poured during a Passover seder, left untouched in honor of Elijah the prophet, who will arrive one day to announce the arrival of the Messiah

etrog (AY-trahg): a type of citrus fruit that is a symbol of Sukkot

gefilte fish (guh-FILL-tuh): a poached mixture of ground fish, served as a Passover appetizer

Haggadah (hah-GAH-dah): the special text followed during a Passover seder

latke (LAT-kuh): a fried potato pancake eaten at Chanukah

lulav (LOO-lahv): a cluster of palm, myrtle, and willow leaves; a symbol of Sukkot

matzoh (MOT-zuh): an unleavened bread eaten during Passover

menorah (meh-NOR-ah): a ceremonial candleholder; the Chanukah menorah holds nine candles: eight for each night of Chanukah and one to light the others

seder (SAY-der): a ceremonial dinner held on the first nights of Passover

shofar (show-FAHR): a ram's horn, blown on Rosh Hashanah to welcome the New Year

sukkah (SOO-kah); plural **sukkot** (soo-KOHT): a small hut built by families in their yards during the Sukkot holiday under which meals are eaten with invited guests

synagogue (SIN-uh-gog): a Jewish house of worship

tallis clips (TAHL-is KLIPS): small clips used to keep the tallis (fringed prayer shawl) in place as it hangs over the shoulders of the wearer